The Princess and the GIANt

FAIRY TALES

BEANSTALKS and other magic plants

BICYCLE REPAIR

BIG Book of BEDTIME TALES

How to TAME YOUR GIANT

For Suzi and George xx
C.H.

To Joanne, Roz, Nadine, Karen and Bex – for all the love, laughs and persistence!
S.W.

First published in 2015 by Nosy Crow Ltd
The Crow's Nest, 10a Lant Street
London SE1 1QR
www.nosycrow.com

ISBN 978 0 85763 387 3 (HB)
ISBN 978 0 85763 388 0 (PB)

Nosy Crow and associated logos are trademarks
and/or registered trademarks of Nosy Crow Ltd.

Text copyright © Caryl Hart 2015
Illustrations copyright © Sarah Warburton 2015

The right of Caryl Hart to be identified as the author
and Sarah Warburton to be identified as the illustrator of this work has been asserted.

A CIP catalogue record for this book is available from the British Library.

Printed in China
Papers used by Nosy Crow are made from
wood grown in sustainable forests.

1 3 5 7 9 8 6 4 2 (HB)
1 3 5 7 9 8 6 4 2 (PB)

The Princess and the GIANT

Caryl Hart

Sarah Warburton

nosy crow

A little princess lived inside
A little tiny house.
Her servant was a tabby cat,
Her butler was a mouse.

Her father made the porridge
And her mother chopped the wood,
And Princess Sophie rode her bike,
Like every princess should.

In the yard, behind the shed,
A magic beanstalk grew.
A giant lived right at the top
(As giants often do).

At night, the giant's stomping
Made the people sob and shake.
"That selfish giant!" Sophie scowled.
"He's keeping me awake!"

STOMP!! STAMP!! SHAKE!!

The princess asked her parents,
"Why are giants mean and bad?"
"Always have been," said her mother.
"Always will be," said her dad.

He found the book of fairy tales
They kept high on a shelf.
"It says so here, in black and white.
Look, read it for yourself."

fairy tales

So Sophie read a story set
In murky days of old,
When Jack climbed up a beanstalk
And discovered piles of gold.

A giant roared, "Get off my stuff!
I'll grind your bones for bread!
I'll FEE FI FO and FUM and then
I'll bop you on the head!"

STOMP!! STAMP!! SHAKE!!

That night poor Sophie tossed and turned.
"Our giant's such a pest.
If only he would go to sleep
We might all get some rest!"

She read about a witch
Who made a house from gingerbread.
It made her tummy rumble
And a plan formed in her head.

At midnight, Princess Sophie
Took some bottles and some packets.
She piled them in her backpack
Then she buttoned up her jacket.

She clambered up the beanstalk.
Brave Sophie didn't stop
Till she reached the giant's castle,
That was balanced on the top.

Suddenly, the giant roared, "Who's creeping round outside?
A nasty little robber! Well, you'd better run and hide!"

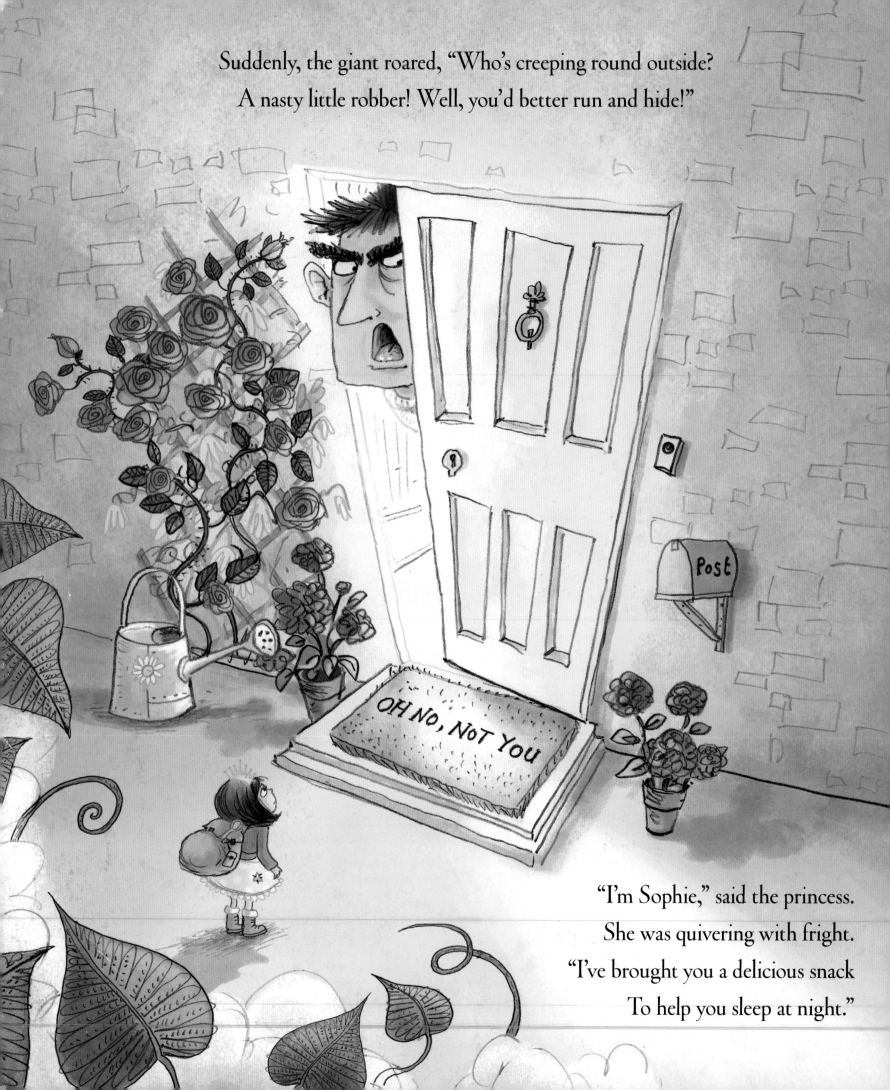

OH NO, NOT YOU

Post

"I'm Sophie," said the princess.
She was quivering with fright.
"I've brought you a delicious snack
To help you sleep at night."

She cooked some lovely porridge
In her father's porridge pot.
"Now, this should help you get to sleep –
It's creamy, sweet and hot."

The giant growled, "This supper
Wouldn't even feed a fly!"
But he ate the porridge anyway,
Then slammed the door. "Goodbye!"

The giant's roars got louder. Sophie ran back home to bed.
She hugged her favourite teddy bear. "I'm glad you're here," she said.

All day long the giant howled. The people ran and hid.
But Sophie had another plan, so this is what she did . . .

She read about a little girl who met three hungry bears,
And wondered whether giants ever felt alone or scared.

. . . she clambered up the beanstalk.
Brave Sophie didn't stop
Till she reached the giant's castle,
That was balanced on the top.

STAMP!!

STOMP!!

SHAKE!!

The giant bellowed, "FEE FI FO! What IS that funny smell?
A horrid little girl has come to trick me, I can tell."
"It's only me," said Sophie, as she held her backpack tight.
"I've brought some cuddly bears in case you're lonely in the night."

Then Sophie made the supper while the giant sulked and huffed.
"Us giants don't need teddy bears! We're strong and brave and tough!"
But he gobbled up his porridge and he drank his milk and honey,
Then he took the biggest bear to bed and squeezed its furry tummy.

But STILL the giant couldn't sleep. The king cried, "Oh my word!
He's making the most dreadful noise that I have EVER heard."
Sophie hugged him tightly. "Daddy, don't be angry, please!
He might be like the poor princess whose bed was full of peas."

STOMP!!

SHAKE!!

STAMP!!

The king and queen were in despair, so Sophie filled a sack.
She dragged it to the garden and she heaved it on her back.
She clambered up the beanstalk. Brave Sophie didn't stop
Till she reached the giant's castle, that was balanced on the top.

The giant called, "FEE FI FO – OH!
It's you again, I see.
I suppose you'd better come inside
And have a cup of tea."

"I have the answer," Sophie cried.
"I know why you're so grumpy.
You can't get any sleep because
Your bed's too hard and lumpy."

She pulled a mattress from the sack
And heaved it on the bed.
She gave the giant blankets
And a pillow for his head.

The giant ate his supper
Then he gathered up his bears
And he went to bed while Sophie
Tiptoed down the castle stairs.

But . . .

. . . the giant didn't sleep at all and soon was in a rage.

The queen cried, "Send the army NOW to lock him in a cage!"

Sophie looked up from her book. She'd tried her very best.

"There's nothing more that I can do," the princess sighed, "unless . . ."

Sophie grabbed her backpack and she scrambled through the door.

"I can't imagine why I never thought of this before!"

She raced back up the beanstalk. Brave Sophie didn't stop

Till she reached the giant's castle, that was balanced on the top.

"Stop that racket!" Sophie yelled.
"And get back into bed!"
The giant was so stunned and shocked,
He did as Sophie said.

The troops swarmed up the beanstalk, and were ready for a fight,
When they heard a sweet and gentle voice that drifted through the night.

"This HAS to work," thought Sophie
As she tucked his teddies in,
And she pulled the softest blanket up
Around the giant's chin.

"Are you sitting comfortably?" they heard the young voice say.
The soldiers stopped to listen and they put their swords away.

Inside the castle, Sophie smiled.

"Oh, how could I forget?

You haven't had a story!

It's no wonder you're upset!"

She pulled the book out from her bag and read a bedtime story.

The giant AND the soldiers were soon fast asleep and snorey.

"I think I've done it!" Sophie gasped.
"Our problems are no more.
The poor old giant couldn't sleep.
Now listen to him snore!"

"He's eaten up his supper and he has some bears to hug.
I've read a lovely story – now he's happy, warm and snug."

To celebrate the happy news, the king announced a feast.
They danced and partied all night long, till ten o'clock at least.
But as the people wandered home, with party bags and cake,
There came a dreadful . . .

THUD! THUD!!

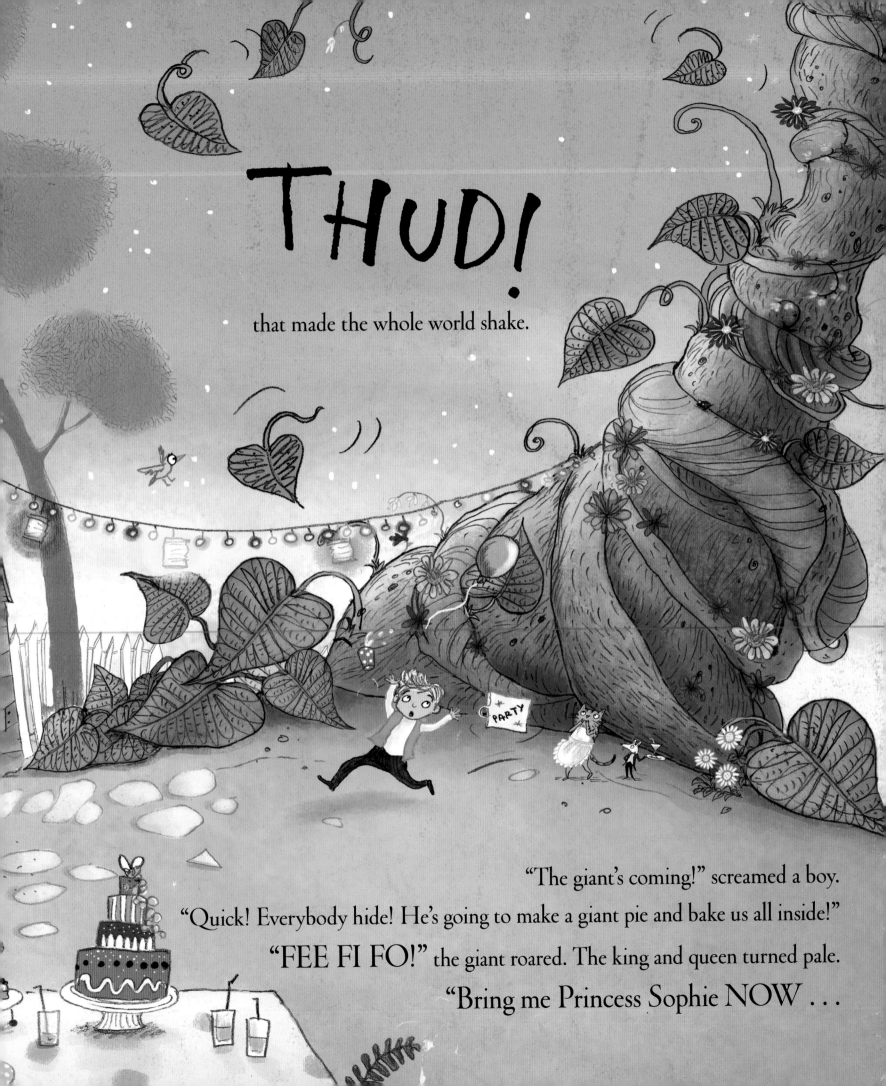

THUD!

that made the whole world shake.

"The giant's coming!" screamed a boy.

"Quick! Everybody hide! He's going to make a giant pie and bake us all inside!"

"FEE FI FO!" the giant roared. The king and queen turned pale.

"Bring me Princess Sophie NOW . . .

. . . I want a fairy tale!"

The people stopped their panicking. They gasped in disbelief.
"Another story?" Sophie smiled, "well, THAT'S a big relief!
But why not read one by yourself?" she asked her giant friend.
"Just start at the beginning and keep going till the end."

"Oh, don't be silly, Sophie!" said the giant with a giggle.
"MY books aren't filled with stories, they're just full of tiny squiggles!"
"Those marks aren't squiggles," Sophie said. "They're words! We call it writing!
This writing tells us stories that are funny and exciting."

Sophie took the giant's hand. "I'll teach you how to read.

But first I need the army's help. There's something that I need."

She sent the giant home to bed, then rubbed her sleepy eyes.

"The next time that we meet," she yawned, "you'll have a BIG surprise!"

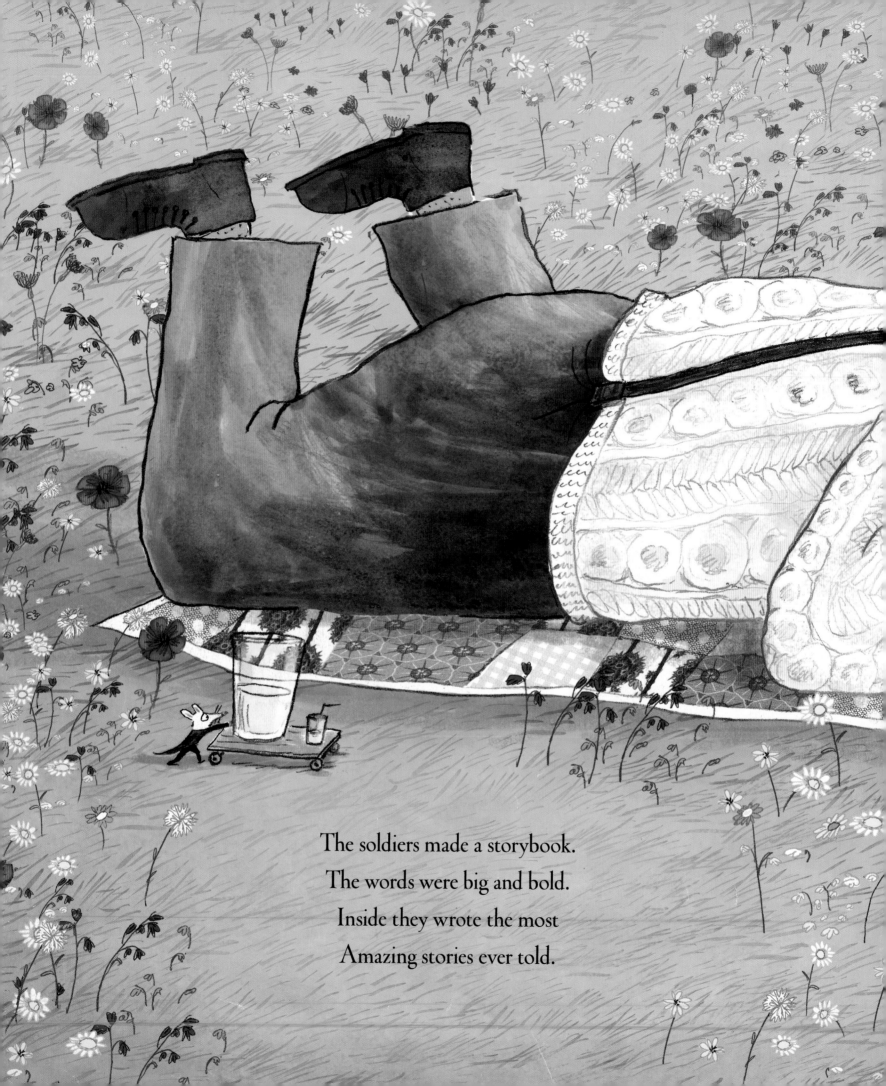

The soldiers made a storybook.
The words were big and bold.
Inside they wrote the most
Amazing stories ever told.

Then Sophie taught her friend to read,
By walking on the lines
And the giant read his giant book,
One word at a time.

From that day forward, Sophie saw the giant every day.
Sometimes they took turns to read, and sometimes they'd just play.
The town was filled with joyful song and happy children's laughter . . .

. . . and the princess and the giant both lived Happy Ever After.

THE END!